Marshmallow Friends

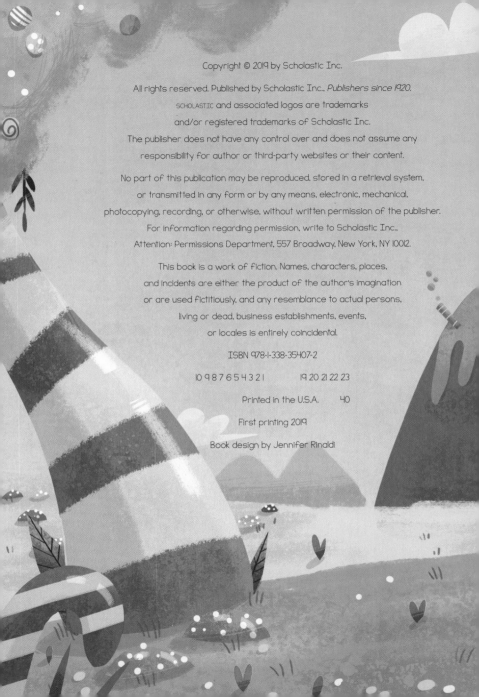

ISBN 978-1-338-35407-2

10 9 8 7 6 5 4 3 2 1   19 20 21 22 23

Printed in the U.S.A.   40

First printing 2019

Book design by Jennifer Rinaldi

Marshmallow Friends

Welcome to the Candy Forest

by Christy Webster

illustrated by
Leire Martín

SCHOLASTIC INC.

Chapter 1

"It's just not right," August said to himself as he tossed another cup of red paint into the trash. He opened his tray of pigments and powders. Then his cabinet of jars and bottles. He'd already tried every shade of red he had, and nothing seemed quite right.

August looked at his painting, then out his window at the Candy Forest surrounding his cottage. The trees, as always, were snow white with swirls of deep, shiny red. They looked good enough to eat. He looked back at his painting again and saw the dull pink, the burnt orange, and the dusty brick of the trees sitting on the canvas. They looked nothing like the beautiful peppermint trees of his home.

There was only one thing left to do. He would ask Sage for advice. Sage was his best friend, and she always had the best advice of anyone in the forest. August had wanted the

painting to be a surprise. But without Sage's help, there might not be a painting at all.

August washed up his brushes, put them away, and walked out into the bright morning sun. It was a little early to go visiting, but he knew Sage was always the first one awake. She wouldn't mind.

He made his way over the winding path through the Candy Forest. The sweet little town nestled among the trees was just starting to wake up. He saw Kai watering her crops, Peyton setting out fresh eggs at the market, and Elliot starting his route with his bag of mail. He waved at each of his neighbors as he passed.

August was already feeling better, walking through town on such a beautiful morning. The sun was as round and yellow as a butterscotch candy. A sweet, cool breeze wove through the sparkling peppermint trees. August's paws squished happily along the coconut dust path. It felt good to move around after staring at his painting for so long. The sound of Baker's Stream nearby was relaxing. And he was sure that Sage would know what to do about his problem.

Finally he reached his best friend's cottage. Most people wouldn't notice it at first—the ginger-brown walls didn't stand out among the brightly colored trees and flowers. But it was the coziest little home in the Candy Forest. August stepped up and gave Sage's shiny blue door a quick knock. The little deer opened it right away, almost as if she had been expecting him.

"I knew you'd be up!" August said brightly. "Good morning!"

"Good morning," Sage replied, smiling.

"But why are *you* out and about so early?"

Sage stood aside so August could enter the little house. It was tiny, but as always, everything was just where it ought to be. Her kitchen shelf had its three teacups and saucers neatly in a row. Her books were lined up perfectly—even though August knew she had probably been reading one just moments before. August loved his own jumble of a house, but there was something about Sage's tidy little home—it reminded him of her.

"I need your advice," August said, and Sage nodded.

"Is your molding clay too soupy?" she guessed. "Guitar strings too tight?"

"Close!" August said, laughing. His best friend knew him well. As long as he was creating something, he was the happiest bear in the Candy Forest. "I'm making a painting, and I can't find the perfect shade of red for the trees." He gestured toward the window at the forest outside.

Sage turned and gazed out at the nearby trees. After a moment, she said, "I can see how that would be hard. I've read hundreds of books and I don't think I've ever seen anything that quite captures the trees of the Candy Forest . . ."

August grinned when he heard Sage trail off. He knew this meant his friend was having an idea.

"Let's go to the library!" Sage blurted out suddenly.

Chapter 2

August nodded and followed Sage out the door. Half of Sage's ideas started with the library, but it wasn't just because she loved to read. Almost every time they went, they came away with something new—an idea of how to solve a problem, a new recipe to use in their Tuesday Best Friend Meals, or an interesting story to pass along.

Sage and August were the first ones at the library, as usual. They greeted Nico, who was sitting at the front desk. Then Sage started pacing through the stacks.

"I know I saw something about paint colors in one of these books," she said. She trailed her hoof along the spines, passing thick books and thin books, old books and new books. Finally she let out a squeak and started pulling a large volume from a high shelf. August helped her get it down and together they carried it to one of the tables in the back.

It was a book about plants and flowers. It was so large August thought it might have information about every plant in the Candy Forest—maybe even the whole world!

"This book has chapters about which plants can be used for food, for medicine, for fabric, for all kinds of things," Sage said. She flipped through quickly, landing on a colorful page showing charts of different plants and the colors that can be made from them.

Sage asked August questions as she read through the chart. "I'm guessing you tried berry juice?" she asked.

"That's what I tried first," August said. "Too pink."

"Oh, how about crushed chestnuts?"

"Too brown."

"What about scorching them a little first?"

"Even browner."

Sage nodded. "Did you try grape juice?"

"Yes, it's much more purpley than the trees."

Sage kept reading. "This says that the best, truest red comes from the ruby plant. The ruby plant is famous around the world for making a dye that looks just like a ruby shining in the sun. Have you ever seen a ruby plant?"

August had never even heard of it. "No. But that sounds just like the shiny red of our peppermint trees! Where do we find one?"

Like a flash, Sage flipped to the back of the
book, skimmed through the index, then turned
back to a page toward the middle. August craned
his neck to get a peek. It was a page all about the
ruby plant. Surprisingly, the picture showed yellow
flowers. Sage must have noticed this too because
she said, "You don't use the flower for the red
dye, you use the root." She pointed to a smaller
picture of the deep red root and read on. "But it
only grows high on mountains. There wouldn't be

any growing anywhere near here."

August was disappointed to leave the library
without a solution. He knew nothing else would
make his painting perfect.

"Perhaps if we boil down the berry juice it will
be less pink . . . or if the crushed chestnuts
could be mixed up with a little bit of the
orange dirt from the riverbed?"

"I just wish I had a ruby root!"
August exclaimed.

"Here you go," said a voice. It was a voice August had never heard before. He turned and saw a stranger— a penguin! She had a colorful cap on her head and a huge pack with dozens of patches in every shape and color.

In her fin, which she was holding out to August, was a bright red root.

Chapter 3

Remy always tried to help folks out when she arrived in a new place. But this was the first time someone had announced what they needed so clearly and so soon after she arrived. If someone needed ruby root, today was their lucky day.

She held it out to the little bear and deer. The bear stared at the root, as if he couldn't believe his luck.

"Where did you get that?" he exclaimed. "It only grows in the mountains!"

"I got it in the mountains," Remy said, smiling. "I'm Remy."

"I'm August, and this is Sage," the bear replied, and the deer tipped her head in greeting. "But the mountains are so far away!"

"Are they?" Remy paused and thought for a moment. She had just been to the Cardinal Mountains right after her hike through the Ivory Desert. Or was it before that? "I travel all the time," she explained. "I go to so many places, sometimes I lose track of the order. But I know I've been to the mountains recently, because the root was near the top of my pack."

She saw August and Sage looking at her big pack curiously. This often happened when she arrived in a new place. Most folks didn't travel very far away from their homes, which meant Remy had the chance to show them treasures they hadn't seen before. It was one of the many things she liked about staying on the road, traveling from place to place.

"I've just arrived in this forest this morning," Remy said. "I have to tell you, I've been to more places that I can count, but I've never seen *anything* like this."

It was true. There was something extra special about this forest, Remy could tell right away. The air smelled fresh and
sweet, like the perfect dollop of whipped cream on a piece of pineapple upside-down cake (her favorite). And the plants and flowers—even the trees—were brightly colored, almost like the hard shell of a sugar sculpture. In fact, ever since she'd arrived, she couldn't stop thinking about sweets.

Sage and August beamed with pride. "This is our home, the Candy Forest," Sage said.

Remy giggled. "It's a good name for it, that's for sure. I would love to stay here a few days and find out more about it."

"Only a few days!" August said, chuckling. "You *must* stay longer than that."

"Oh, no!" Remy protested. "I always keep

moving. It's what I do. I never stay in one place very long. I like to travel, meet new friends, see new places, learn new things—"

At this, Sage's ears pricked up. She had already been eyeing Remy's pack even more than August, but now she was practically jumping in anticipation.

"Would you . . . would you like to see some of the things I've picked up recently?" Remy offered.

"Yes!" Sage exclaimed.

Remy removed her pack and placed it on the path in front of her. "Will you hold this?" she asked August, and handed him the ruby root. He held it carefully with both hands, as if it were made of glass.

Then Remy unlaced the top of her pack. She lifted out the item on top, a small basket. "This is called an aam basket. It comes from the Verdant

Jungle, which I traveled through on my way here," Remy explained. "The grasses are woven so tightly that you can carry water in it without spilling a drop!" She handed the basket to Sage, who dipped it in the nearby stream and drank from it.

Sage's eyes went wide. "But this tastes . . ."

Remy nodded. "Not only can it hold the water, the grass gives it a refreshing mango flavor."

"Delicious!" Sage exclaimed.

Then Remy reached in her pack and pulled out a folded cloth. "The same mountain range where I found the ruby root was full of fluffy sheep that grew the softest wool I've ever touched," she said. "But you have to be careful with it. It makes blankets and pillows so soft and snuggly that you fall asleep as soon as you get into bed." She unfolded the cloth and handed a corner to August.

He reluctantly held the root in just one paw and took the cloth in the other.

"Careful, August!" Remy warned, seeing his eyelids already starting to droop.

August quickly placed the corner back in Remy's fin and resumed holding the root with both paws. "Wow," he said.

"And that's just the beginning!" Remy said. "My pack is full of things I've carried on my back from far and wide. You never know what could help someone out in the next place I visit. Like your root there."

August gasped. "My root?"

"Sure," Remy said. "You said you needed one. I don't usually get such specific requests, but I'm happy to be able to help."

"Is that why you travel around so much?" Sage asked. "To bring folks things they wouldn't find where they live?"

"It's one of the reasons," Remy replied. "But the biggest reason is just that traveling is my favorite thing in the world to do."

"But how can I take this?" August sputtered. "It's too valuable."

"It's only valuable to someone who has a use for it!" Remy replied. "You need to make red dye or paint?"

"The reddest," August said.

"Well then," Remy said, putting the other treasures back in her pack.

"But I have to give you something in return!" August said.

Remy settled the pack back on her shoulders. "I'm glad you offered. Because I know just the thing. You can *both* help me, in fact. I need something very valuable from you."

Sage and August waited.

Remy smiled. "A tour around the Candy Forest," she said.

Chapter 4

Sage was more than happy to give Remy a tour of the Candy Forest. It was very rare to have a new friend visiting. And Sage was proud of her home—it felt good to show it off.

"We should probably start at the library," Sage suggested. "It's my favorite, and it's right here."

"Back so soon?" Nico asked when he saw Sage. She knew he wasn't surprised to see her, though—this wasn't the first time she'd made two visits to the library in one morning.

He did look surprised, though, when Remy followed August in.

"This is my favorite place in the Candy Forest, other than my own house," Sage explained to Remy. "There's always something in these books that I didn't know before."

The shelves went on and on, showing spines in every color of the rainbow.

Sage could tell Remy was impressed.

"Maybe you don't need me to bring things from far away after all!" Remy said. "With this many books, you could look up anything you need!"

"Oh, there's no such thing as too much knowledge!" Sage protested. She knew Remy's pack held just as many surprises and treasures as a freshly cracked book—not to mention everything she could tell them about faraway places and people. "I can't wait to find out every detail about your travels!"

"You will," Remy promised. "But first I want to

see the rest of the Candy Forest!"

They continued through the little town, introducing Remy to their neighbors wherever they went. Ila at the orchard showed off her candy and caramel apples. Remy marveled at the colorful foil-covered eggs at Peyton's market. At the edge of town, Remy gazed at Baker's Stream tumbling over the rocks, through the trees, and out of sight.

When they got to the
repair shop, Dede burst
out the front door.
"How did you know?"
she asked.

Sage was confused.
"How did I know what?"

"Not you," Dede said. "August!
How did you know I finished your frame early?"

August started. "My frame! I've spent so much
time thinking about finding the perfect red, I
almost forgot it was here." He turned to Remy to
explain. "Dede runs the woodwork shop. I knew
I'd need the perfect frame for my painting once
I finished. I came here because Dede is an
expert woodworker."

"Who's this?" Dede asked,
suddenly noticing Remy.

"This is Remy," Sage said. "She's a visitor from far away!"

"How far away?" Dede asked.

"I come from a place so far south that it's covered in snow," Remy told her.

Sage couldn't believe it. She'd never seen snow before. She wondered what it was like. August looked like he was thinking the same thing.

"But I have been on the road for as long as I can remember," Remy said. "I've traveled to every kind of place there is."

"Not to a place like this," Dede said with a question in her eyes.

Remy agreed, gazing toward the pale brown checkered pattern of Dede's shop. It came to a point at the top and was surrounded by pink, white, and brown flowers. "Your shop reminds me of an ice cream cone, somehow. Why *is* the Candy Forest so . . . sweet, anyway?"

August smiled. "Because the folks who live here are so sweet!"

"I can see that," Remy said, and laughed.

"Thank you for my frame, Dede," August said. "It will be perfect for my painting. Sage, can we show Remy my house next so that I can drop it off?"

They said goodbye to Dede and continued to August's house. He hurried inside to cover his painting before letting Sage and Remy in. "It's going to be a surprise," he said.

While they waited, Sage saw Remy examining the colorful shingles that made up the outside of August's house. While her own house was a simple ginger brown and frosty white, August's had been built with every color imaginable—no two shingles were the same.

"These shingles remind me of something," Remy said. She breathed in slowly. "Sugar cookies? Or . . . maybe these special candies my uncle used to make me for my birthday." She shook her head, looking lost in thought.

To Sage, August's house simply made her think of August. Her best friend was always bouncing from here to there, making creations as varied as the colors of these shingles. But he was always there for her.

August came out and led his friends into his kitchen, putting away his new frame and placing the ruby root carefully on top of his fruit bowl. Then he showed Remy his fluffy bed covered in pillows, his cabinet bursting with art supplies, and his little guitar. To Sage, the house looked messy—it always did. But she could tell August had tidied up a little for Remy.

After that, they circled back through the peppermint trees and across Baker's Stream to Sage's cottage. All the pieces of art August had made for her over the years were neatly arranged, as always. And she proudly showed off her most favorite thing—her own little collection of books. "Sometimes I read one so many times that Nico lets me keep it," she explained proudly. "As long as I let someone else borrow it if they need it."

"I can't believe how beautiful this place is!" Remy said. "You both must love living in the Candy Forest!"

"We do!" August said. "Now, where are *you* going to live, now that you're here?"

"Oh!" Sage exclaimed. She loved having a project. Finding the perfect spot for a new home, choosing the best materials to build with—this was going to be great. "Yes, can we please help you build it?" she asked, clapping her hooves together. "I'm very organized, and August is so creative—he'll make it look pretty."

Remy laughed and lifted her fins in protest. "Don't forget! I'm only staying here for a few days. I'm sure you would build a lovely house, but I don't need one."

Sage had already forgotten that Remy was planning to move on soon. The three of them were getting along so well, it was like they had always been friends.

"I guess we'll have to find something else to do today," Remy said.

"That's easy," August said.

"Yes," Sage agreed. "It's Tuesday."

"What's so special about Tuesdays?" Remy asked.

Sage and August looked at each other and smiled. Just at that moment, August's stomach growled.

Chapter 5

"Tuesday is Best Friends Meal Day!" August said, giggling. "Every Tuesday Sage and I cook lunch and dinner for each other and eat together."

"What a nice tradition," Remy said. "But I don't want to intrude on your special day together. I'm sure I can find something else to do."

"Are you kidding?" Sage said. "You are the inspiration for my dish today!"

"Mine too," August agreed.

"Besides," Sage added, "a little change in routine is just right, now and then. You'll see."

"Okay," Remy said. "Thank you."

"Yay! I've got lunch this week!" August said. "I can't wait to make it for you."

"And I've got supper," Sage said, rubbing her hooves together in anticipation.

"Wait," Remy said. "If you are making lunch, and you are making supper, what can I make?"

"Hmm . . ." Sage tapped her nose, thinking.

Normally, Sage was the problem-solver, but this time, August knew exactly what to do. "You can make dessert!" he exclaimed.

"Oh, that's perfect," Remy said, looking around. "I've had sweets on my mind all morning. Should I make a pie? Cookies?"

"Make it a surprise!" August said. "We always do."

Remy nodded and the three friends went back to the market.

"Best Friends Meal Day?" Peyton asked when they walked in. "Feels like it was just Tuesday."

"Lucky us!" August said,
and made his way to the vegetable section. He
saw Remy duck into the pantry section, and Sage
zipped directly over to the icebox.

August loved shopping for vegetables. His
favorite part was seeing the bottom of his basket
get more and more colorful as he went along.

First he picked out a bright yellow sweet
pepper. Then a pretty white head of garlic. A

bright green cucumber, a dark green spicy pepper, and a nice, round pink onion joined them in his basket. With every new color, August felt more and more inspired. For August, cooking his Tuesday meal for Sage was just as creative as painting or sculpting or playing his guitar. That's why he loved it.

Finally he got to the tomatoes. He picked out the reddest tomato he could find. He thought about how he'd tried to make red paint out of tomato skins a few days earlier. But no matter what he'd done, it always came out too orange. He felt grateful all over again that Remy had given him her ruby root. He looked over at Remy, who was lifting a sack of sugar into her basket. Suddenly he couldn't wait to work on his painting again.

"One masterpiece at a time, August," he told himself, and finished his shopping.

A short while later, they were at August's house, unpacking their groceries.

"But how are we going to keep our dishes a surprise?" Remy asked. "We're all cooking together in the same kitchen."

"We may get a clue here or there," August said. "But we don't look at the finished dishes until it's time to eat."

"Besides," Sage said. "August has the biggest, best kitchen in the Candy Forest. Everyone would make their meals here if they could."

August beamed. "A work of art needs the right canvas," he said, and glanced over at his painting nook.

The three friends got to work cooking. August was so focused on his lunch dish, he didn't even have time to guess what Sage and Remy were making. He chopped and smashed and mixed his vegetables. The green, yellow, pink, and white

swirled together in a big bowl of red. It looked
just as pretty now as he had imagined when he
was shopping.

Before he knew it, his dish was done and it
was time to eat. Sage had already set the table
and Remy was just sitting down when August
served lunch.

"It's gazpacho!" August announced. "It's in your
honor, Remy, as our special guest."

"In my honor?" Remy looked touched, and also a little confused.

"It's cold vegetable soup," August explained. "Cold, like the place you come from, way down south. Ever since you mentioned it, I couldn't stop thinking about my favorite cold dish."

"Awww," Remy said, clapping her fins together lightly. "That is so sweet."

August smiled. Just then, his stomach growled again.

"Also, I love gazpacho," Remy added, laughing. "Let's eat."

The soup tasted just as good as it looked. As he was eating, August's mind turned back to his painting. He hadn't gotten the chance to work on it all day. And his Best Friends Meal Day duties were almost done. He wondered . . .

"August," Remy said, as though she'd read his

mind, "I have some free time while a piece of my dessert bakes. Once we're done cleaning up lunch, would you like to make some red dye from the root?"

"Yes!" August exclaimed. "I might be able to finish my painting this afternoon!"

While Sage got back to work on supper, Remy and August washed up the lunch dishes and got to work on the red dye. August chopped the ruby root into little pieces while Remy set a pot of water to boil. Before long, they had a big pot of mush—but it was the brightest red mush August had ever seen.

"Finally!" he exclaimed. "Thank you, Remy!"

"Would you mind if I used some of this?" Remy asked. "This dye is edible, and I think it might be just the right finishing touch to my dessert."

August knew all about finding that perfect finishing touch. They split the mush into two bowls and he hurried off to his painting, being careful to angle his canvas so that his friends couldn't see it . . . just yet.

He was so lost in his work that he was surprised when Sage announced it was time for supper already. But as soon as he stood up he realized he was indeed hungry again. He went to the table and couldn't believe his eyes.

Chapter 6

Sage's supper was the opposite of August's colorful gazpacho. While the soup had been a colorful mishmash of vegetables, Sage's table was neat and orderly—and every single thing on it was white. There was tofu, rice, cauliflower, and tall glasses of cold milk at each place.

"This supper is in honor of our new friend Remy!" Sage said.

"Thank you, Sage," Remy said, but she was a little unsure what it all meant.

"It's white—just like the snowy place you come from," Sage explained. Remy looked again and saw Sage was right—the whole table looked like a snowy field.

Remy put her fins over her heart and lowered her head. "Thank you so much." Then she took a bite, and her eyes popped open. "How did you get so much flavor in this tofu, Sage? By looking at it you would think it was completely plain."

August grinned. "Everything Sage makes tastes great, no matter how it looks. Just like everything I make looks great, no matter how it tastes."

"But your gazpacho was so good!" Remy protested.

"That's true," Sage said. "But you never tasted the dim sum he tried to make one time."

August laughed out loud. "They were pretty!"

"Pretty bland," Sage said.

The three friends laughed and joked while

they ate Sage's delicious supper.
Finally it was time for dessert.

"My new friends," Remy said
before unveiling her creation.

"I have traveled all around the world, and I have never felt as welcome anywhere as I do here in the Candy Forest. I've also never been to a place that could serve as a better inspiration for a dessert."

Then Remy went to the kitchen and brought out her surprise—it was a gingerbread village, but not just any gingerbread village. It was

August's colorful house, Sage's simple cottage, and peppermint trees, re-created with warm spicy gingerbread, fluffy white frosting, and colored candies. And, of course, the tree was the exact perfect shade of red.

Sage and August loved it.

Remy had meant what she said about feeling more welcome here than anywhere else she had traveled. She couldn't believe how thoughtful

Sage's and August's separate meals had been. Remy's love of travel didn't stop her from thinking fondly of her childhood home. She *did* miss the snow, and the cold — sometimes. She could tell Sage and August had really wanted to help her feel at home in the Candy Forest.

And she did. More than any place since she'd left the snowy South Pole.

As the three friends ate their dessert, the sun sank below the horizon, looking almost as red as the shiny red tree trunks. When a beam of light hit August's face through the window, he jumped out of his seat and said, "I have one more surprise! Wait here while I get it ready!"

Chapter 7

"It's *just* right!" August said to himself, clapping his fluffy paws together and admiring his painting once again. He'd spent the afternoon putting the finishing touches on it, but it had been Remy's red pigment that had made the difference. He couldn't wait to show it to her.

He arranged the painting just how he wanted it—in front of the window facing east. That way, it would have the backdrop of the red and white trees outside his house, but without the light from the setting sun coming in too bright behind it. He

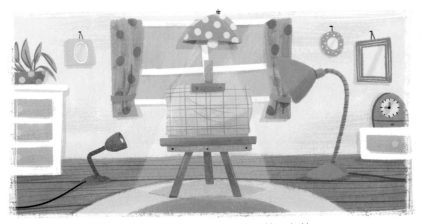

carefully arranged his lamps so that there was plenty of light falling exactly where he wanted it. Then he very gently draped a pillowcase over the painting and called his friends in from the kitchen.

August clapped his paws together. The moment was finally here! This was one of his favorite parts of the creative process—showing his work to people—especially when he knew that they would like it. Sage was always supportive of his artwork. But even though he had only known Remy for one day, he knew somehow that she would be the same way.

August nudged Sage and Remy into the perfect spots to view the painting, then double-checked that the lamps were just where he wanted them to be.

"Remy, if you had not arrived in the Candy Forest today, this painting would not have been the same," August said, preparing to lift the pillowcase off. "And not just because I wouldn't have had the right shade of red."

With that, he drew the pillowcase away and revealed the painting. He didn't take his eyes off the faces of his two best friends.

As soon as August lifted the pillowcase off the painting, Remy knew that she'd made a decision.

The painting, perfectly encased by the new frame Dede made, took place outside in the

Candy Forest. Even with the ruby root that she'd brought from the mountainside, Remy didn't know how August could have gotten the trees to look so real. They were creamy white with swirls of deep shiny red. They looked hard but delicate as though they were made out of sugar, with the light shining through them just so. Looking at them, Remy could almost taste the flavor of peppermint.

Standing among the trees, smiling, August had painted himself, Sage, and . . . Remy.

"August!" she cried. "How could you have done this so quickly? We only just met today!" She stepped closer and looked at the smaller version of herself on the canvas. "It looks just like me!"

"It sure does," Sage agreed.

August beamed with pride. "It's a painting of me and my friends. I wanted to capture the special day we had together."

Tears sprang to Remy's eyes.

"You don't like it?" August asked, a worried look appearing on his face for the first time since Remy had met him.

"Of course I like it!" Remy said, and August sighed with relief.

How to explain? Remy had traveled all over the world and met countless people. Most of them had been very friendly, and Remy had loved meeting them and trading stories. But she usually moved on so quickly, she couldn't remember the last time she had been called "friend."

"I was just thinking, Sage," Remy said.

"Yes?" Sage replied.

"I've only gotten to show you a few of the things in my pack," Remy said.

Sage nodded eagerly.

"And, August, I'd love to describe to you some of the places I've been."

"That would be a great idea for my next artwork!" August exclaimed. He hurried to his cabinet and pulled out his pencils and sketchbook, as if he couldn't wait a moment to get started.

"And you have that library, with all those books," Remy continued. "It will take me a lot more than a few days to read them all."

"What are you saying?" Sage asked.

"Well . . . maybe I should stay a bit longer than I'd planned, here in the Candy Forest," Remy finally said.

"I knew it!" August exclaimed.

Remy continued. "You know I'm always looking for more adventure, and I just have the feeling that there is a lot more adventure to be found here."

Sage was looking at her with eager eyes. "And can I . . . ?"

"Yes! Of course, Sage, you can help me build my house," Remy said. "I have learned a lot on the road, but I've never stayed in one place more than a few days. So I've never built a house. I don't know the first place to start."

"I do!" Sage exclaimed. She produced a notebook from somewhere and started making a to-do list.

"And I know the first piece of artwork you can hang in your new place once it's finished," August said.

"You do?" Remy asked. August just smiled and

looked at the painting he had revealed this morning.

"Really?" Remy said. "But you worked so hard on this!"

"It's for you," August said. "But you might have to teach me more about going on adventures. That way I can go to the mountains and find more of that ruby root for future projects."

Remy thought about that. Having company on an adventure? She'd always traveled on her own before now.

Then she thought, a little change in routine might be just right, now and then.